To my daughter Bria, the inspiration for everything I do.
- Mr. Jay

For my sunshine and my tiger
- Erin

New Paige Press, LLC
NewPaigePress.com

New Paige Press and the distinctive ladybug icon are registered trademarks of New Paige Press, LLC

ISBN 978-0-578-19803-3

Printed and bound in China

New Paige Press provides special discounts when purchased in larger volumes for premiums and promotional purposes, as well as for fundraising and educational use. Custom editions can also be created for special purposes. In addition, suuplemental teaching material can be provided upon request. For more information, please contact sales@newpaigepress.com.

Ricky, the rock that couldn't ROLL

written by **Mr. Jay**   Illustrated by **Erin Wozniak**

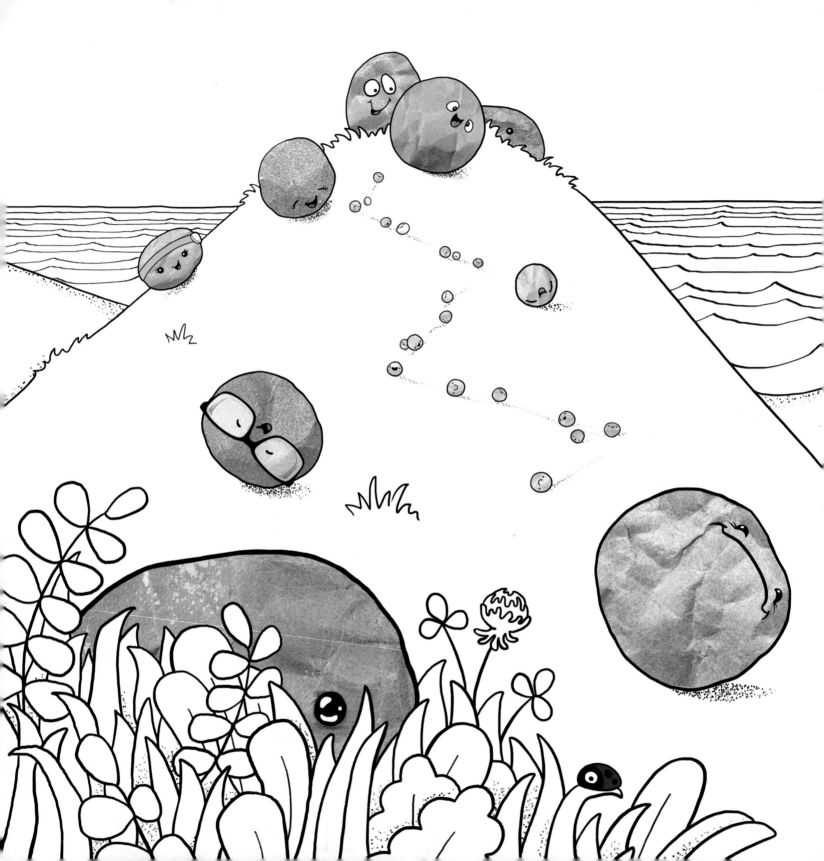

Over the lake and out past the bay
was a green, grassy hill where the rocks came to play.

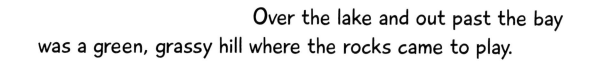

They would race to the top to take in the view,
then roll their way down, the way rocks love to do.

There were Kip, Pip, and Chester, and Marvin the Boulder.
Ignatious played too, though he was much older.
And a group called "The Pebbles" never, ever sat still,
zig-zagging their way up and over the hill.

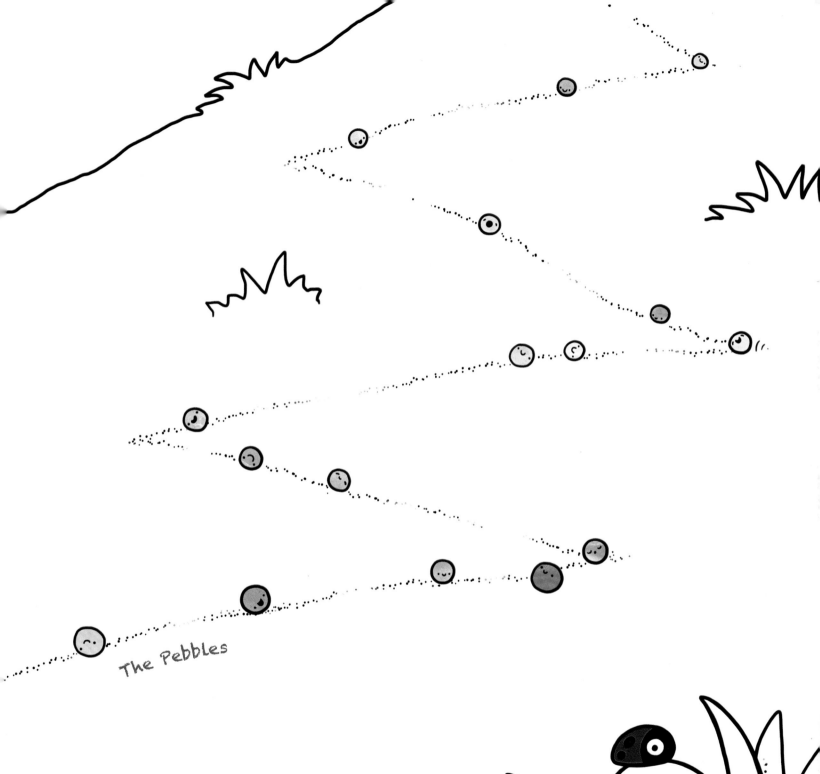

The Pebbles

Kai was a meteorite and not from this planet,
and Maya was lava but taken for granite.

Stu was the smart one; Parker, the clown;
and grumpy old Ebert rolled 'round with a frown.

Gabby was sassy; Leesie had flair;
Emma was giggly and Hud had black hair.

But the one trait that seemed to be shared by them all
was that every rock there was shaped like a ball.
And because they were round, they could easily roll,
through the grass, past the lake, up and over the knoll.

Except for poor Ricky, who quietly sat.
You see, Rick couldn't roll because one side was flat.

His friends didn't get it.

"Come roll!"

they would chant.

So Ricky tried, but replied, "I'm sorry, I can't."

But the rocks were determined, they were sure they could solve
Ricky's flat-sided problem, and help him revolve.

So Marvin the boulder, with his impressive physique,
carried Rick all the way to the hill's grassy peak.

Then he pushed him downhill, yelling,

"Keep rolling, kid!"

but Rick didn't roll -
he just kind of slid.

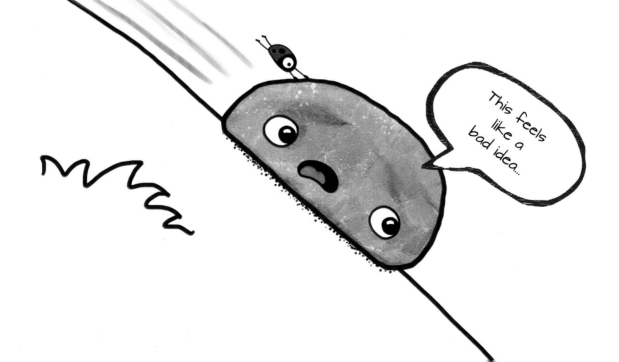

Boing!

Boing!

GLUE

Well, the rocks weren't done - not by a mile.
Surely, this next try would get Rick to smile!
They stuck rubber balls all over Rick,
using big gobs of glue to get them to stick.
They were proud of themselves,

"This will work!"

they announced.

But Ricky still couldn't roll - now he just sort of bounced.

Well, they pushed and they pulled, trying every which way,
to get Rick to roll, but by the end of the day,
nothing had worked, just like Rick expected,
and he ended up feeling depressed and dejected.

"It's no use,"

Ricky sighed,

"There just isn't a way.
So I'll sit off to the side,
and watch you all play."

But his friends wouldn't quit.

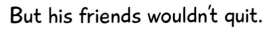
"We're here for you, brother,
and we'll get you to roll, one way or another."

So they pondered and thought,
each straining his brain,
'til they looked up and saw
it was starting to rain.

And that's when it hit
that smart stone named Stu.

"Eureka!"

he shouted, **"I know just what to do!"**
He explained to them how
they would get Rick to tumble.

"My plan is pure genius!"

(Stu wasn't too humble.)

So they carried our hero down the road 'bout a mile,
to the lake where they gathered up mud they could pile,
on the flat side of Rick, creating a mound,
that they shaped, smoothed, and sculpted, until it was round.

Then after the rain, with the sun in the sky,
they left him to bake 'til the mud was all dry.
They gathered up vines and one colorful feather
that they wrapped all 'round Rick, to keep it together.

When the last knot was tied, and the work was all done,
the only step left was for Rick to have fun.

They stood back and watched, feeling nervous and tense,
as Rick breathed in deep, with increasing suspense.
He moved slowly at first, testing out his new mold,

and then,

for the first time...

Ricky the rock...

ROLL!

So Bria, the ladybug, who'd been there from the start,
felt a surge of pure joy swell up in her heart.
She thought, as she watched her friends play on the hill,
that there's always a way if there's also a will.
And she said to herself, as Ricky rolled down the slope,
"When you're surrounded by love,
you always have hope!"

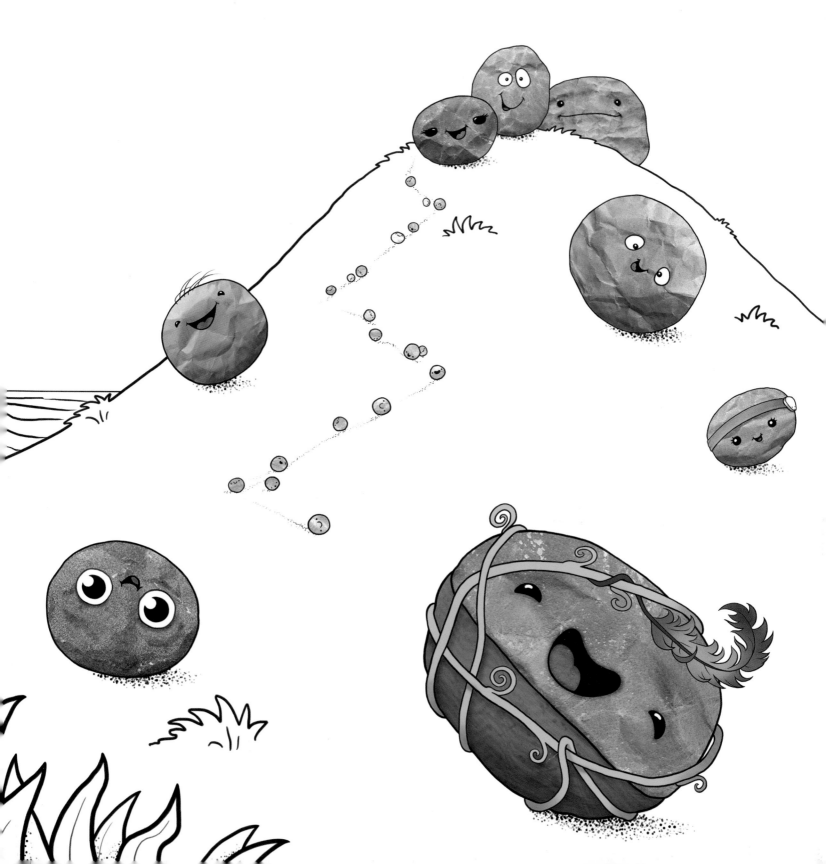